T0407785

BLACK VOICES ON RACE

JORDAN PEELE

by Shasta Clinch

FOCUS READERS

NAVIGATOR

WWW.FOCUSREADERS.COM

Focus Readers is distributed by North Star Editions:
sales@northstareditions.com | 888-417-0195

Produced for Focus Readers by Red Line Editorial.

Content Consultant: Peter Ukpokodu, PhD, Professor of African and African-American Studies, University of Kansas

Photographs ©: Jordan Strauss/Invision/AP Images, cover, 1; Shasta Clinch, 2; BFA/Alamy, 4–5; Shutterstock Images, 7, 15, 18–19, 23; PictureLux/The Hollywood Archive/Alamy, 8–9; Danny Moloshok/Invision for the Television Academy/AP Images, 11; Chris Pizzello/Invision/AP Images, 12–13; Charles Sykes/AP Images, 17; iStockphoto, 21; Blumhouse Productions/Universal Pictures/Monkeypaw Productions/Album/Alamy, 24–25; Red Line Editorial, 27; Jim Bourdier/AP Images, 29

Library of Congress Cataloging-in-Publication Data
Names: Clinch, Shasta, author.
Title: Jordan Peele / by Shasta Clinch.
Description: Lake Elmo, MN: Focus Readers, [2023] | Series: Black voices on race | Includes index. | Audience: Grades 4-6
Identifiers: LCCN 2022000080 (print) | LCCN 2022000081 (ebook) | ISBN 9781637392676 (hardcover) | ISBN 9781637393192 (paperback) | ISBN 9781637394199 (pdf) | ISBN 9781637393710 (ebook)
Subjects: LCSH: Peele, Jordan, 1979---Juvenile literature. | African American comedians--Biography--Juvenile literature. | African American actors--Biography--Juvenile literature. | African American screenwriters--Biography--Juvenile literature. | African American motion picture producers and directors--Biography--Juvenile literature. | Racism--United States--Juvenile literature. | United States--Race relations--History--Juvenile literature.
Classification: LCC PN2287.P36 C55 2023 (print) | LCC PN2287.P36 (ebook) | DDC 792.702/8092 [B]--dc23/eng/20220224
LC record available at https://lccn.loc.gov/2022000080
LC ebook record available at https://lccn.loc.gov/2022000081

Printed in the United States of America
Mankato, MN
082022

ABOUT THE AUTHOR

Shasta Clinch is a freelance copy editor and proofreader. She lives with her husband and two lovely littles in New Jersey.

TABLE OF CONTENTS

CHAPTER 1
Get Out 5

CHAPTER 2
Getting In 9

CHAPTER 3
Rising Star 13

CHAPTER 4
Changing the Narrative 19

CHAPTER 5
Unfolding a New Story 25

A CLOSER LOOK
Systemic Racism 28

Focus on Jordan Peele • 30
Glossary • 31
To Learn More • 32
Index • 32

FROM THE MIND OF JORDAN PEELE AND
BLUMHOUSE THE PRODUCER OF THE VISIT, INSIDIOUS & THE GIFT

GET OUT

JUST BECAUSE YOU'RE INVITED, DOESN'T MEAN YOU'RE WELCOME.

CHAPTER 1

GET OUT

In the movie *Get Out*, a man meets his girlfriend's family for the first time. He is Black. The family is white. Scary things start happening to the man. He learns that the white people want to live forever. And they know how to do so.

First, they kidnap young, healthy Black people. Then they put their own minds

Daniel Kaluuya was nominated for Best Actor for his performance in *Get Out*.

into the Black people's bodies. The man must leave before he loses his body, too.

Jordan Peele wrote and **directed** *Get Out*. It was one of the biggest movies of 2017. In 2018, *Get Out* was up for four Academy Awards. Peele won for Best Original Screenplay. This award honors the storytellers who write the movies. Peele was the first Black **screenwriter** to win this award.

Peele gave an acceptance speech when he received the award. He thanked everyone who had given him a voice and helped make the movie happen. He also thanked his mother. She had taught him to love even when faced with hate.

In 2017, Jordan Peele made *Time* magazine's list of the world's 100 most influential people.

Peele's win showed that he had a powerful point of view. Viewers cared about what he had to say. And they liked how he said it. Many people were excited to see what he would do next.

IN
LIVING

CHAPTER 2

GETTING IN

Jordan Peele was born on February 21, 1979, in New York City. His mother was white. His father was Black. Jordan didn't see his father very often. His mother raised him alone.

Jordan watched a lot of TV shows and movies growing up. He enjoyed shows with funny **sketches**. He also studied

One of Jordan Peele's influences was *In Living Color*. This comedy show included funny sketches, dancing, and rap music.

scary movies. These movies and shows inspired him to try acting. Later, while in college, he discovered improv comedy.

Improv is short for improvisation. Performers have to come up with their lines without a **script**. And they have to listen carefully to one another. They must respond to what their partners are saying.

BLACK AND WHITE

In New York City, being **biracial** was not unusual. But Jordan still often felt out of place. For example, he had dark skin. People would see him with his white mother and be shocked. The experience taught him about other people's expectations. He learned he had to adapt.

For Peele (right), improv is best when partners listen to each other.

By doing so, they can work together to create an unplanned and hilarious show.

For Peele, improv was a chance to play many different kinds of people. When he was younger, he had worried about sounding wrong. Specifically, he'd worried about talking "white." But with improv, Peele could never sound wrong. The whole point was to act in different roles.

CHAPTER 3

RISING STAR

Jordan Peele left college after two years. However, he kept doing improv. In 2002, he did a show at the famous Second City theater in Chicago, Illinois. There, Peele met Keegan-Michael Key. Key was another improv actor. Later, they both worked on a TV show called *MADtv*. The show often did **satire**. Peele and Key

Jordan Peele (left) and Keegan-Michael Key immediately worked well together as a comedy duo.

played many famous Black people on the show.

After a few years, the two men created a new TV show called *Key & Peele*. On that show, they used comedy to explore problems in American society.

SATIRE ON *KEY & PEELE*

"Gay Wedding Advice" is a sketch from *Key & Peele*. Peele plays a man whose cousin is getting married. The cousin is gay. Their family has questions about what a gay wedding is like. So, they ask a gay man. The man tries to explain that a gay wedding is just like any other wedding. But the family keeps asking questions. And the questions are very inappropriate. They show some of the false beliefs some people have about gay people.

Peele has worked with many comedians, including Tracy Morgan (right).

The sketches made people think about important topics. These topics included **racism**, **homophobia**, and gender.

For example, one of the most popular sketches was in the first episode of the first season. It was about US president Barack Obama. Obama was known for his calm speech. But in the sketch, Obama explains that he does get mad. He just shows it in a different way. To help people understand, he uses an anger translator. A translator is someone who changes words from one language into another. Obama's anger translator expresses how the president really feels.

In the sketch, Peele acts as Obama. Key plays Luther, Obama's anger translator. While Obama speaks in his usual calm way, Luther paces and yells angrily. This sketch explored the way the real Obama behaved in public. It also explored how many Black people feel they have to act. They must adapt to the expectations

Obama (left) and Luther were very popular characters. They appeared in many sketches on *Key & Peele*.

many white people have. They must behave one way in public and another way in private.

Key & Peele ended after five seasons. By then, Peele was ready to try something different.

CHAPTER 4

CHANGING THE NARRATIVE

When Jordan Peele was 13, he dreamed of becoming a horror movie director. He made this dream a reality with *Get Out*. Peele got the idea for the movie after Barack Obama was elected the first Black president. Peele felt that many people thought racism was over. He worried that people thought

As a director, Jordan Peele worked with actors to get the best results for the film.

it wasn't important to talk about race anymore. So, he made a horror movie that focuses on race.

For example, *Get Out* begins with a Black man nervously walking in a white neighborhood at night. For Black people, this is a regular discomfort they

FROM COMEDY TO HORROR

Going from comedy to horror might seem hard. But Peele didn't think they were that different. Both can be based on real life. And both can make people uncomfortable. With horror, Peele felt he could still comment on society, but this time without using laughs. So, he decided to write and direct horror movies.

Black people might feel out of place or too visible in mostly white, suburban neighborhoods.

experience. But because *Get Out* is a horror movie, other viewers are worried, too. Another example involves Chris, the main character. Chris asks his white girlfriend if her family knows he's Black.

In addition, the way Chris is treated in the movie is important. The girlfriend's mom sends Chris's mind to a deep, dark, and scary place. She does this so the family can use Chris's body. The way a white person controls Chris is a reminder of slavery. Peele wanted to show how slavery still affects Black people today through systemic racism. This idea says that organizations and laws affect people of color in an unfair way.

Peele also wanted to show that even people who seem supportive can end up being the bad guys. Chris meets many white people at his girlfriend's family home. They all seem nice. They say positive things about race. But they are all part of the plan to take Chris's body.

In *Get Out*, Chris is treated as a useful body instead of as a person. This is like how enslaved people were treated.

Peele wanted all viewers to enjoy the movie. But he especially wanted Black audiences to like it. For many people, the movie was **revolutionary**. The main actor played a big role in this. People of color weren't usually the stars of horror movies. But *Get Out* stars a Black man.

WARD

CHAPTER 5

UNFOLDING A NEW STORY

Jordan Peele continued to act after *Get Out*. But after the movie's success, he focused on directing. The next film he directed and wrote was *Us*. It is about regular Americans who have to fight off terrifying clones of themselves. The movie features a Black family. But it is not about race. Instead, it's about class.

In *Us*, a well-off family is haunted by a struggling family that looks just like them.

Peele said people often feel they deserve their advantages. In doing so, they ignore the suffering of others. Peele also believed it is important to tell stories about Black people that aren't about race.

In addition to directing, Peele focused on **producing**. His company produced movies and shows that lifted the voices of people of color. For example, *The Twilight Zone* is a new version of an old show. It includes many horror, mystery, and science fiction tales. Like *Key & Peele*, it addresses racism, immigration, and other current topics. *Lovecraft Country* is a horror show set in the American South in the 1950s. A Black family searches for a missing man. On the way, they find many types of monsters.

Peele's works address key social issues. And they highlight the importance of showing diversity on-screen. His stories can inspire everyone to have necessary conversations about American society.

JORDAN PEELE TIMELINE

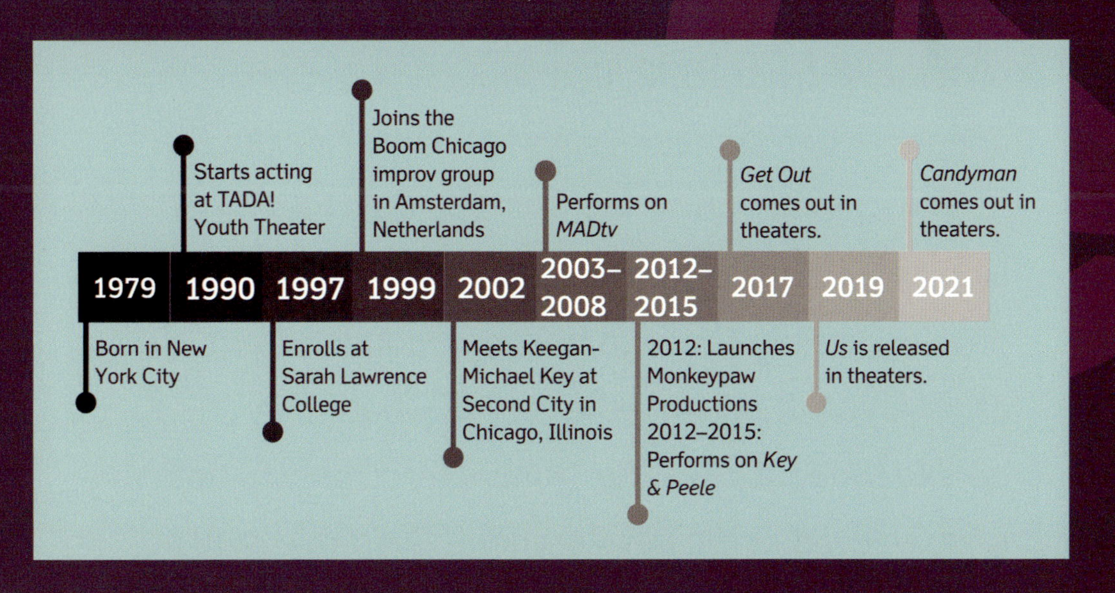

SYSTEMIC RACISM

The United States was founded on slavery. Slavery was outlawed after the US Civil War (1861–1865). But the idea that people of color are less important is built into all parts of society. For example, people of color are often mistreated at schools and at hospitals. They are treated unfairly when they look for jobs and homes.

Jordan Peele coproduced and cowrote *Candyman*, which came out in 2021. It is based on a movie from 1992. It is about a ghost who appears when someone says his name five times.

The original movie featured the Cabrini-Green Homes. Cabrini-Green was a real housing development in Chicago that was isolated from other areas. It became the face of what many people thought of as the "inner city." Many people of color lived in the development. Systemic racism

The huge high-rises of Cabrini-Green housed thousands of people. The buildings were often poorly built.

made it hard for them to find good homes. The new *Candyman* is set in the neighborhoods where Cabrini-Green once stood.

FOCUS ON
JORDAN PEELE

Write your answers on a separate piece of paper.

1. Write a paragraph that describes the main ideas of Chapter 4.

2. Do you think comedy or horror is a more effective way to comment on society? Why?

3. Which movie or show did Jordan Peele direct?

   A. *MADtv*
   B. *Us*
   C. *Lovecraft Country*

4. How could satire help bring awareness to difficult social problems?

   A. By poking fun at racist or homophobic actions, it could make people think.
   B. By showing scary monsters, it could make people afraid.
   C. By sharing funny jokes, it could make people laugh.

Answer key on page 32.

GLOSSARY

biracial
Having parents from two different races.

directed
Was in charge of making a movie.

homophobia
Hatred or mistreatment of people because of their sexuality.

producing
Managing a movie and raising money to pay for filming.

racism
Hatred or mistreatment of people because of their skin color or ethnicity.

revolutionary
Capable of producing great change.

satire
A work that makes fun of human behavior with comedy.

screenwriter
A person who writes the script for a movie or show.

script
The written form of a movie, including what actors say.

sketches
Short plays or acts, especially funny ones.

TO LEARN MORE

BOOKS

Bell, Samantha S. *Jordan Peele*. North Mankato, MN: Capstone Press, 2018.

Green, Amanda Jackson. *Diversity and Entertainment: Black Lives in Media*. Minneapolis: Lerner Publications, 2021.

Harris, Duchess, and Tammy Gagne. *Race and the Media in Modern America*. Minneapolis: Abdo Publishing, 2021.

NOTE TO EDUCATORS

Visit **www.focusreaders.com** to find lesson plans, activities, links, and other resources related to this title.

INDEX

Academy Awards, 6

Cabrini-Green Homes, 28–29
Candyman, 27, 28–29

directing, 6, 19–20, 25–26

Get Out, 5–6, 19–23, 25, 27

horror, 19–23, 26

improv, 10–11, 13, 27

Key, Keegan-Michael, 13–14, 16, 27
Key & Peele, 14–17, 26–27

Lovecraft Country, 26–27

MADtv, 13–14, 27

Obama, Barack, 15–16, 19

producing, 26, 28

racism, 15, 19–20, 22, 26, 28

satire, 13
sketches, 9, 14–16

The Twilight Zone, 26

Us, 25, 27

writing, 6, 20, 25, 28

Answer Key: 1. Answers will vary; **2.** Answers will vary; **3.** B; **4.** A